First published 2000 in *The Macmillan Treasury of Nursery Stories*
This collection first published 2010 by Macmillan Children's Books
a division of Macmillan Publishers Limited
20 New Wharf Road, London N1 9RR
Basingstoke and Oxford
Associated companies throughout the world
www.panmacmillan.com

ISBN: 978-0-230-74998-6

A CIP catalogue record for this book is available from the British Library.

Printed in China

MACMILLAN CHILDREN'S BOOKS

Snow White
and other stories

Retold by
Mary Hoffman

Illustrated by
Anna Currey

Snow White

Once upon a time a beautiful queen sat sewing at her window. It was winter and her ebony window framed a landscape all white with snow. The queen pricked her finger and, as the bright blood welled up, she thought, "How I wish I had a little girl whose skin was as white as snow, whose hair was as black as ebony and whose lips were as red as this blood!"

And, by the end of the year, the queen's wish came true, for she gave birth to a baby girl, whose skin was as white as snow, her hair black as ebony and her lips red as blood.

But it was a hard birth and the queen died of it. The king was very sad and he called his little daughter Snow White.

Time went by and the king was lonely, so he married again. His second wife was a beauty, too, but a very vain one. She had a magic mirror in her bedchamber and every morning she spoke to it:

"Mirror, mirror, on the wall,
Who is the fairest one of all?"

And the mirror would reply:

"The loveliest creature ever seen
Is none but you, O gracious queen!"

The queen was not fond of Snow White, who grew prettier with every day. So imagine her shock when, one day, she asked her mirror, "Who is the fairest one of all?" and heard this reply:

"She who makes the darkness bright,
The lovely princess called Snow White."

The queen was furious, but she knew that the mirror never lied. So she made a terrible plan. She called the palace's chief huntsman to her and told him to take the child into the forest and kill her.

"And when you've done it, bring me her lungs and liver as proof!" said the wicked queen.

The huntsman went to call Snow White to join him for a walk in the forest. She went with him happily because she knew all the people who worked in the palace and they were all nice to her. As they got deeper among the trees, the huntsman thought he really couldn't kill the sweet, pretty girl. So he told her about the queen's orders. "Run away, Snow White," he said, "and God keep you safe."

But he secretly thought she would probably be killed by wild beasts anyway.

As he travelled back to the palace, the huntsman killed a wild boar and took its lungs and liver to the queen.

"So, it is done," she said. "Tell the cook I'll have them for supper."

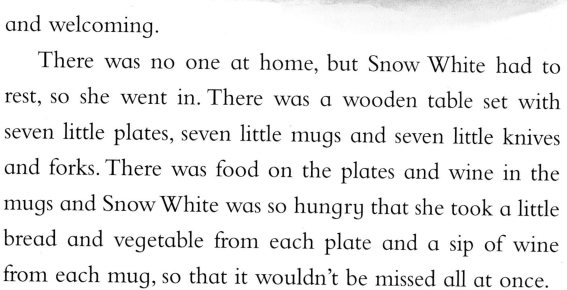

Snow White was very scared alone in the forest. But no animals harmed her and, in the end, she came to a little cottage with smoke coming out of the chimney, which looked cheerful and welcoming.

There was no one at home, but Snow White had to rest, so she went in. There was a wooden table set with seven little plates, seven little mugs and seven little knives and forks. There was food on the plates and wine in the mugs and Snow White was so hungry that she took a little bread and vegetable from each plate and a sip of wine from each mug, so that it wouldn't be missed all at once.

Then she saw seven little beds lined up against the wall. She was so tired that she wanted to go to sleep in one of them, but one was too short, one too soft and one too lumpy. She tried them all and the seventh one seemed the most comfortable, so she snuggled under the covers and fell fast asleep.

When it grew dark, the owners of the house came

home. They were seven dwarves, who worked in the mines all day, digging out copper and gold. As soon as they got inside they knew someone had touched their meal and they could see dents in their beds. But the seventh dwarf found a little girl fast asleep in his!

The dwarves gathered round to admire the sleeping child. They were kindly creatures and thought they had never seen anything so lovely as Snow White. At that moment, she woke up and saw seven little faces with white beards, looking down at her. She told them her story, about how her stepmother had wanted to kill her and how she had run away.

"That's all right, my dear," said the dwarves. "You'll be safe with us, as long as you don't let anyone into the house. You can stay here and we'll look after you but, in

return, you must do all the cooking and cleaning and tidying of the house."

"I'd like that," said Snow White.

When they had eaten their supper, they went to bed and the seventh dwarf slept one hour in each of the other dwarves' beds so that Snow White could have his.

Back at the palace the next morning, the queen asked her mirror:

"Mirror, mirror, on the wall,
    Who is the fairest one of all?"

But the mirror replied:

"O Queen, you are fairest of all I see,
    But over the hills, where the seven dwarves dwell,
    Snow White is still alive and well,
    And none is as fair as she."

Then the queen knew she had been tricked and plotted even harder to get rid of Snow White. She disguised herself as a pedlar-woman and went to the dwarves' cottage.

Snow White was happily dusting and sweeping while the dwarves were at the mines, when she heard a voice calling, "See my lovely ribbons and laces. Pretty things for pretty girls." Snow White couldn't resist and she opened the door. The pedlar-woman stepped in and said, "Wouldn't you like to buy yourself something nice as a treat after all your housework? How about this lace?"

And she showed Snow White a rainbow-coloured lace for her bodice. "Here, let me thread it for you," said the old woman, and she laced Snow White so tightly into her bodice that she couldn't breathe and fell down on the floor.

When the dwarves came home they thought their little friend was dead. But they quickly cut the rainbow lace and Snow White could breathe again. She told them what had happened. "But that must have been the wicked queen," they said. "You must be on your guard and not let anyone in the house."

Back at the palace, the queen asked the mirror her usual

question. But the answer came:

"While Snow White breathes and shows her worth,
    She's still the fairest on this earth."

The queen ground her teeth with rage and thought how she might kill her enemy. She knew all sorts of witchcraft and disguised herself again to look like a quite different old woman. Then she put poison on a hair comb and set out for the dwarves' cottage.

Snow White was baking an apple pie when she heard a voice saying, "Who would like something pretty for her hair?" Snow White opened the door and saw an old woman with a tray full of bows and slides and pretty combs.

"I know just the thing for you," said the old woman, holding out the poisoned comb. "Just think how these sparkling stones will set off your dark hair."

And Snow White was so fond of sparkly things that she let the pedlar in. The old woman showed her the comb and put it in her hair. Immediately, the poison entered Snow White's skin and she fell down in a swoon. But luckily it was nearly time for the dwarves to come home and, as soon as they found her, they drew the comb out of her hair.

Snow White sat up, well as ever and anxious to get her pie in the oven. But the dwarves were very worried. "You really must promise not to open the door to anyone," they told her. "The queen is determined to kill you."

Back at the palace, the queen spoke to her mirror and it said:

"The loveliest creature alive tonight
Is the beautiful princess called Snow White."

The queen tore her hair with fury. She used all her witchcraft to make a poisoned apple. It was red on one side and white on the other and looked as tasty as an apple can be, but one bite from the red side was deadly.

Then the queen turned herself into a farmer's wife and went to the dwarves' cottage.

Snow White was making a pair of curtains when she heard a voice call, "Apples, apples, nice sweet apples!" Now, Snow White was

very fond of apples, but
she knew she mustn't open
the door. So she opened
the window instead. How
delicious the apple looked
that the farmer's wife was
holding out to her!

"Apple, my pretty?" asked the old woman.

Snow White shook her black hair. "I'm not allowed," she said.

"Whyever not?" said the old woman. "They're good and wholesome. Look, I'll take a bite myself." And she bit out some juicy flesh from the white side of the apple. Then she held out the red side to Snow White. The little girl couldn't help herself. She took a bite.

Immediately, Snow White fell down dead and the witch queen ran happily back to the palace. When the dwarves came home, they could not revive Snow White. They looked for laces and combs but didn't think to look inside her mouth. Sadly, they agreed that she must be dead, but she still looked so beautiful that they couldn't bear to bury her. So they made a glass coffin and put Snow White in it, and put it on a hilltop nearby. One of

the dwarves watched over the coffin every day.

The queen was happy at last in her palace, for whenever she asked the mirror,

"Mirror, mirror, on the wall,
  Who is the fairest one of all?"

it replied:

"The loveliest creature ever seen
  Is none but you, O gracious queen."

And she was very happy that her rival was dead at last.

As for the dwarves, they missed Snow White very much. She didn't change a bit, keeping her rosy cheeks and her white complexion. Years went by and, one day, a young king was out hunting in the hills. He saw the glass coffin and immediately fell in love with the beautiful girl who seemed to be sleeping in it. He spoke to the dwarf who was on guard by the coffin and heard the whole of Snow White's story.

The king begged and pleaded with the dwarves to let him take the glass coffin back to his kingdom, so that he could continue to gaze at the girl. He offered them a large heap of gold in return. At first they wouldn't hear of it, but he seemed so broken-hearted that eventually they said yes.

The king had the coffin put on a carriage pulled by horses but as they set off through the forest, the first horse stumbled on a tree root. The coffin slipped off and fell on the ground, tipping Snow White out. And, with that, the piece of poisoned apple was dislodged from her mouth. She woke and found herself looking into the eyes of a handsome young man.

In a moment the king was on his knees asking Snow White to marry him, and she was happy to say yes. She said goodbye to the seven dwarves and went to live with her king in his kingdom. The invitations soon went out to a grand wedding.

Now, when Snow White's wicked stepmother got her invitation, she spent days getting herself ready. When she was dressed in all her finery, the wicked queen asked her mirror:

"Mirror, mirror, on the wall,
　Who is the fairest one of all?"

and got this reply:

"Of all ladies here you the loveliest are,
　But the new young queen is fairer by far."

The queen turned pale with fury. But she was even more furious when she arrived at the wedding and saw that the bride was Snow White! She was so angry that she couldn't move. All her magic froze up inside her and she turned to stone. Snow White lived happily with her king and she had the wicked queen moved to the park where she made a beautiful statue for the birds to sit on.

The Frog Prince

Long, long ago, when wishing was useful, there lived a king with a very beautiful daughter. She was so used to everyone telling her that she was lovely as the day that, to be truthful, she had become rather vain and silly and inclined to think that everyone should do as she said.

By the castle was an old dark forest and, at the edge of it, in the castle grounds, was a tall shady lime tree. Under the lime tree was a well of clear cool water beside which the princess liked to sit, playing with her golden ball.

One day, she was sitting by the well tossing the ball up

in the air and catching it, tossing it up and catching it, tossing it up and . . . oh! dropping it down the deep, deep well! The princess sprang to the rim of the well and looked down, but it was no good. She couldn't even see the bottom, let alone her golden ball. How she wept and wailed!

"What's the matter, princess?" said a deep voice. "You cry so hard that even a stone would have pity on you."

The princess looked up and saw a large frog sticking his big ugly head out of the well.

"Alas," she said, through her tears. "I have dropped my golden ball down the well and it is so deep that I shall never get it back."

"Don't say that," said the frog. "I could get your plaything for you, but I'd want something in return."

"Anything!" said the princess, clapping her hands and quite cheerful again. "My clothes, my jewels, why, even my little golden crown."

"Pah!" said the frog. "What good are such things to me? I can't wear your clothes or your jewels and a frog would look silly in a crown. What I want is for you to love me and let me be your companion. Will you let me eat off your golden plate and drink from your golden cup and sleep in your golden bed?"

"Yes, yes, of course," said the princess, impatiently.

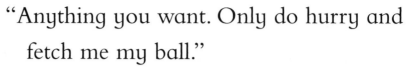

"Anything you want. Only do hurry and fetch me my ball."

The frog disappeared into the water in a shower of bubbles and was back in a trice, carrying the ball in his wide mouth. He spat it out on the grass and the princess, delighted to have her plaything back, wiped it on her silk gown and skipped back to the castle to change her clothes.

And did she thank the frog? No. Did she remember her promise to him? No. The poor frog hopped wetly after her, crying, "Wait for me, wait for me!" while the princess never even looked back.

As she was sitting down to supper with the king her father, there came the strangest sound, of something creeping splish, splash, splish, splash, up the grand marble staircase. There was a knock at the dining-room door and a deep voice said, "Princess, princess, let me in!"

Startled, the princess opened the door, but shut it again

quickly when she saw the lumpy bumpy face of the frog looking up at her. She went back to her place with a racing heart and flushed face.

"Why, whatever is the matter, my dear?" asked the king. "Is there a giant outside the door?"

"No, Father, it is not a giant, but just a disgusting old frog."

"A frog, my dear? What does a frog want with you?"

"Today, my golden ball fell in the well and the frog got it back for me. And . . . and he made me promise he could be my companion in return. But I didn't imagine he could leave the well. And now here the horrid thing is."

And she started to cry some very small crystal tears which just wet her long lashes and made her eyes look pretty. But, to her astonishment, her father gave her a very stern look.

"A promise is a promise," said the king. "No matter to whom you make it."

And he made the princess open the door and let the frog in. The frog hopped slowly up to the table, for he was tired after his long journey from the well.

"Lift me up beside you," he cried.

The princess shuddered, but her father was still watching her seriously, so she did as the frog asked. Her lumpy bumpy new companion pushed his mouth into her golden plate and dipped his long tongue into her cup. And, strangely, the princess lost all her appetite and ate and drank no more of her supper.

When the frog was full, he said to the princess, "I am very tired. Now take me to your bedroom and let us both lie in your golden bed."

At this, the princess began to cry in earnest, for she hated the idea of the cold wet frog in her clean and comfortable bed. But the king was angry with her. "The frog kept his side of the bargain," he said. "Now you must keep yours."

So the princess held the frog at arm's length, from the tips of her fingers, and carried him to her room, where she put him in a corner. Then she went to bed and cried herself to sleep.

She was woken by the clammy frog trying to climb into her bed.

"Lift me up!" he said, "or I shall tell your father."

So she did.

"Now, princess, if you are my loving companion, as you promised," said the frog, "you must kiss me goodnight."

How the princess screwed up her pretty eyes so that she might not see him and how she screwed up her pretty nose that she might not smell him and how she screwed up her pretty mouth that she might not taste him! And she gave the frog the quickest little peck of a kiss that she could get away with.

There was a rushing sound in the room and, when the princess opened her eyes, there was no frog to be seen.

Instead of his ugly warty face, there gazed back at her the handsomest prince she had ever seen!

Immediately, he went down on one knee.

"Thank you, thank you, beautiful princess," he said. "You have broken the spell. A witch changed me into a frog and condemned me to live in that cold dark well, until a beautiful princess released me with a kiss."

Imagine the princess's confusion! But her father had told her she must be a loving companion to the frog. So the princess suddenly discovered she was very obedient and married her frog prince and lived happily ever after.

The Three Billy Goats Gruff

Once upon a time there were three goat brothers who lived in a field together. They spent their days munching the long green grass and then skipping and playing around in their field.

But one day, they noticed that the grass in the field didn't look so green any more.

"Look," said Great Big Billy Goat Gruff. "We've eaten all the best grass. It seems much greener in that field there over the wooden bridge."

"That's right," said his brother, Middle Billy Goat Gruff. "That grass is much lusher and juicier than ours."

"So why don't we go there?" said their baby brother, Little Billy Goat Gruff.

"Mmm," said Great Big Billy Goat Gruff. "It's not as simple as that. You see, there's a bad old troll living under that bridge. He tries to eat everyone who crosses over."

"Then we must think of a plan," said Little Billy Goat Gruff.

Next morning, the bad old troll was sleeping under his bridge, when he heard the sound of hooves trit-trotting across the wooden planks.

"Goodie," he thought. "Here comes breakfast. I haven't

had anything to eat for days."

And he started to sing a horrid little song:

> "I'm a troll,
> fol-de-rol,
> I'm a troll,
> fol-de-rol,
> I'm a troll,
> fol-de-rol—
> And I'll eat you for my breakfast!"

And he leapt out from under the bridge to pounce on Little Billy Goat Gruff who was trit-trotting over the wooden bridge.

Little Billy Goat Gruff's heart was pounding, but he bravely stood his ground.

"Please, Mr Troll," he said, "I don't think that's a good idea. You see, I'm only a little kid and I wouldn't make much of a meal for you. In fact, I wouldn't be more than a mouthful. Why don't you wait for my big brother? He'll be along in a minute and he's much bigger than me."

The hairy troll scratched his head.

"Well, all right. If you're sure he's coming soon."

And he let the little kid trot on over the bridge and into the new field.

The troll spent a very hungry morning until he heard the sound of some more hooves clip-clopping over the wooden bridge.

"Aha!" thought the troll. "That little kid was telling the truth. My tummy will soon be full."

And he started to sing his song again:

"I'm a troll,
fol-de-rol,
I'm a troll,
fol-de-rol,
I'm a troll,
fol-de-rol—
And I'll eat you for my dinner!"

Out jumped the troll and there was Middle Billy Goat Gruff halfway across the bridge. He looked much meatier than his little brother.

"Oh, Mr Troll," said Middle Billy Goat Gruff. "You don't really want to eat me. I'd only make a snack for a large troll like you. Why don't you wait for my big brother, who will be coming along soon?"

The troll was really hungry now, but he was also very greedy and he liked the idea of eating an even bigger goat. So he let the middle brother go clopping on his way across the bridge and into the other field.

All afternoon the troll listened out for the sound of his goat meal trying to cross the bridge but all he could hear was the rumbling of his own tummy. And then, at last, when the sun was going down, the bridge started to tremble and the sound of hooves came stomp-stamping over the wooden bridge.

Aha! thought the troll and out he leapt, singing:

"I'm a troll,
fol-de-rol,
I'm a troll,
fol-de-rol,
I'm a troll,
fol-de-rol—
And I'll eat you for my supper!"

When he saw Great Big Billy Goat Gruff, the troll's mouth began to water. The other goats had been right: there was plenty of eating on their big brother. But what was this?

The big goat wasn't frightened by the troll and his song. Great Big Billy Goat Gruff lowered his big head, with its big horns, and charged. He butted the troll high up into the sky . . .

Over the fields . . .

Over the hills . . .

. . . and right over the sun, till he was quite out of sight. And the bad old troll was never seen again.

Then Great Big Billy Goat Gruff stomp-stamped on his way, over the wooden bridge, and joined his brothers in the field where the grass was green as green. And for all we know, they are living there still.